Runaway

Pete Guppy

SURVIVAL

RISING ★ STARS

in association with

NASEN House, 4/5 Amber Business Village, Amber Close, Amington, Tamworth, Staffordshire B77 4RP

Rising Stars UK Ltd.
22 Grafton Street, London W1S 4EX
www.risingstars-uk.com

Text © Rising Stars UK Ltd.

The right of Pete Guppy to be identified as the author of this work has been asserted by him in accordance with the Copyright, Design and Patents Act, 1988.

Published 2009

Cover design: Roger Warham
Cover image: Courteney Lanier/Alamy
Text design and typesetting: Roger Warham
Publisher: Gill Budgell
Editorial consultant: Lorraine Petersen

All rights reserved. No part of this publication may be reproduced, stored in a retrieval system or transmitted in any form by any means, electronic, mechanical, photocopying, recording or otherwise without the prior permission of Rising Stars UK Ltd.

British Library Cataloguing in Publication Data.

A CIP record for this book is available from the British Library.

ISBN: 978-1-84680-597-4

Printed in the UK by CPI Bookmarque, Croydon, CR0 4TD

Mixed Sources
Product group from well-managed
forests and other controlled sources
www.fsc.org   Cert no. TT-COC-002227
© 1996 Forest Stewardship Council

Chapter 1

"Stop nagging me!" yelled Joe.

"I'm not nagging you," said Mrs Barker.

"Yes, you are, so shut up," said Joe, as he ran up the stairs to his bedroom.

Mrs Barker came to the bottom of the stairs and shouted, "What did you say to me?"

Joe stopped at the top of the stairs and looked back.

"I said, stop nagging me. My dad never nagged me like you do!" he shouted.

Then he slammed the door of his bedroom.

Mrs Barker ran up the stairs and pushed open the bedroom door. "Well, you are not living with your dad. You are living with us. So just do as you are told," she said.

Joe was sitting on his bed. He was holding a bottle and looking at the ship that was inside it.

"Just shut up and leave me alone," he said.

Mrs Barker went red in the face. "How dare you speak to me like that? Just wait until I tell Mr Barker when he gets home from work. He'll deal with you. And you know what that means!"

Then she slammed the door and went downstairs.

"Now I'll get a telling off from Barker. And I might get a slap as well," said Joe to himself.

He sat thinking about why he was living with the Barkers at all. He was there because his mum was dead and his dad was away at sea.

His mum had died in a car crash when he was six years old. They had been going on holiday when a van came round a bend too fast and crashed into them.

His dad had looked after him. But he worked on the boats and was away at sea a lot of the time. So that's when he stayed with his gran.

He had loved living with his gran. But she was too ill to look after him now and lived in an old people's home. That's why he was living with the Barkers.

His dad had said, "Look, Joe. I'm going to sea just one more time. When I come back I'm getting a job on land. I've asked Mr and Mrs Barker to look after you, so be a good lad. I'll be back in six months time."

That was just after his 12th birthday. His dad had given him a bottle with a ship in it as a birthday present.

It was a great present. He had always wanted one. It was a old sailing ship with three masts and sails made of silk. Joe had wanted to know how they got it inside the bottle.

His dad had said, "I'll tell you how they do it when I come home."

But he hadn't come home. And now Joe had been with the Barkers for over two years.

Living with the Barkers had been OK for the first six months. They were pleased to get the money his dad sent them because Mr Barker only had a part-time job.

Then his dad sent a letter from Hong Kong saying he had a new job that would pay him a lot more money. He didn't say what the job was but he said he would be home soon.

Then the letters and the money stopped coming. And the Barkers didn't like it.

No one knew where his dad was. And as time went on, it was clear that the Barkers didn't want him around. Mr Barker had started drinking too much and sometimes slapped him. Mrs Barker nagged him about everything.

Joe sat on his bed looking at the bottle. It made him ask the same old questions. "Where was his dad? Why had his letters stopped coming? Why hadn't he come back home?"

There was one question Joe didn't want to ask. "Was his dad still alive?"

Tears began to fill his eyes. He told himself to stop thinking like that. He knew what he had to do. He had to get away from this house and go looking for his dad.

Chapter

2

Joe had made up his mind to run away.
But did he have the guts to do it? Then he
began thinking about the night Mr Barker
came home drunk from the pub.

He had looked at Joe and shouted,
"Let me tell you something about your dad.
He's left you here for good. He's making a
lot of money and having a good time. He's

stopped sending us the money we need to keep you, and he's spending it on himself."

Mr Barker opened a bottle and took a swig. Then he shouted, "And I'll tell you something funny about your dad. Your no-good tramp of a dad went to sea on a boat called *The Tramp*. That's right. He's a tramp on *The Tramp*."

Joe had run at Mr Barker and tried to hit him. But Mr Barker had seen him coming and slapped him across the face. It was a night Joe would never forget.

His mind was made up. He pulled out a bag from under his bed. Then he tiptoed to the door and put his ear to it.

Good. Mrs Barker was still downstairs.

He opened the bag and took out all the things that were inside. He hoped he had everything he needed to stay on the run.

He had a sleeping bag. A small gas stove to cook on. A pan for his food.

A torch for the dark. A penknife. A fishing line in case he needed to catch his own food. A box of matches and a big plastic sheet for putting over him when it rained.

They were the things he'd used on camping trips with his dad.

He put them all back in the bag. Then he put in a shirt and some pants. Had he got everything? No! He needed cash.

Joe went to the drawer by his bed and got out the money he had saved up.

He grinned to himself. He had got some of it out of old Barker's wallet when he was too drunk to know what was going on.

He put the money in his jacket and went to the bedroom door again.

Mrs Barker was going out to do her Saturday shopping. He heard the door slam as she left. She was still in a bad mood.

Joe put his jacket in the bag. He was just shutting the bedroom door when he stopped.

The bottle! He had forgotten the ship in the bottle. It was the last thing his dad had given him.

Joe picked it up and put it in the bag. Then he ran downstairs to the kitchen. He grabbed some tins of beans, a tin opener and a small dish. He picked up a bottle of water and some bread. Then he got some ham and cheese from the fridge. Joe zipped up his bag.

He was ready to go and he could feel his heart pounding. Could he do it? Could he stay on the run? Or would the Barkers and the police track him down?

Then he thought about his dad and how much he wanted to find him. Joe picked up his bag.

He opened the front door and stepped out onto the street.

Chapter

3

Joe had a plan. He would walk 12 miles to the nearest town. From there he would hitch a lift to Liverpool. That's where he would get himself onto a boat going to Hong Kong.

He'd go from being a runaway to a stowaway. No one had seen or heard from his dad after he had changed his job in

Hong Kong. He had to get there and start asking questions. He didn't know if he could get onto a boat without being seen, but he was going to try.

Joe couldn't risk getting a lift from his village to town in case someone knew him and started asking questions. His plan was to walk the 12 miles on footpaths, staying well away from roads. He knew the first two miles of paths because he had been on them before. He had looked at the rest on a map at school.

He set off, and was soon leaving the village behind him. He had a smile on his face. He was happy to be free of the Barkers. And every step was taking him closer to his dad.

It was a lovely spring day and the sun felt warm on his back, 12 miles didn't seem far to go. But getting over the stiles was hard work.

The bag seemed to be getting heavier and the handle was cutting into his hand. Sometimes there was barbed wire on some of the stiles and it took longer to get over.

When he saw St. Mark's Church he knew he had walked three miles. But it had taken two hours! It was taking him far too long.

He stopped for a drink of water. The thundering of hooves told him he wasn't alone in the field. A herd of cows came running over to take a closer look at him. Big eyes and wet noses crowded round him. They stuck out long, wet tongues trying to lick him.

Joe picked up his bag and made a run for it. The ground shook as the cows chased after him. Joe sprinted to the next stile. He threw his bag over and dived after it.

He hit the ground hard and stayed there.

When he got his breath back, he got up. Looking at the cows he said, "The next time I see you, I hope you're in a pie."

He walked on for the next two hours. Then he got lost! It took him an hour to find the path again. It was now 4 p.m. and the sky was turning black.

"I hope that storm isn't coming my way," said Joe to himself. It was. Big drops of rain turned into a shower. Joe dashed across to an old barn for shelter.

He was just in time as the shower turned into a downpour. Then came the hailstones and thunder. The storm didn't last long but the rain kept falling.

"It's going to be dark soon and I'm still miles from town. I'll get soaked if I walk in this," he said to himself.

So he settled down for a night in the barn. He drank some water and ate his ham and cheese.

The rain stopped as the night began. A full moon shone its light on the fields and barn. Joe got into his sleeping bag and shut his eyes. He opened them again when the noises started.

First, a scratching from high up in the barn, then a snuffling sound close to his head.

Three short, sharp barks made him get out of his sleeping bag. Just outside the barn was a fox, sniffing around for food.

Then he saw something that made no noise at all. A barn owl flew out of the barn. Its wings looked ghostly white in the moonlight.

"Fantastic. This is better than seeing it on TV," Joe said to himself.

Joe got back into his sleeping bag but didn't get much sleep. It was 9 a.m. when he got up. He had made up his mind what to do.

It was taking him too long to get to town. He was going to have to risk getting a lift.

It took him an hour to get from the barn to the road. He didn't have long to wait before a car came along. The driver stopped and opened a door.

Joe was about to jump in when he saw who the driver was. It was Mr Morgan, a man who lived in his village.

"Hello, Joe," he said. "What are you doing out here?"

Joe had to think quickly. Had the Barkers gone to the police yet? Did anyone in the village know he was missing?

"I've been staying with a friend on a farm. I need a lift into town," he said.

"Come on, then," said Mr Morgan. Joe got into the car and put his bag on his lap.

"That's a big bag, Joe. What have you got in it?" asked Mr Morgan.

"Oh, just a few things," he said.

Joe could see Mr Morgan looking at his bag now and then. He felt trapped.

Were all his plans going to come to an end, right now?

When they got to town Mr Morgan stopped the car. He said, "Look Joe, is there anything you want to tell me?"

"What do you mean?" said Joe.

"Well, I know you are not very happy at home. And here you are on the road with a bag in your hand. I think you are running away," said Mr Morgan.

Joe grabbed his bag, opened the door, and ran.

"Come back, Joe! I want to help you. Come back!" yelled Mr Morgan.

Joe kept running. "I'm a prat," he said to himself. "I should never have got a lift so close to home. Now the Barkers and the police will know where to come looking for me."

Joe slowed down to a walk. He had
to think.

How long had he got before the Barkers
went to the police? Two hours? Three hours?
Maybe they would wait to see if he came
home by himself. That would give him
more time to get away.

All he had to do was find the road going
to Liverpool. He could hitch a lift and get
out of this town. Then he saw an ice-cream
shop. He just had to have one.

"I'll just sit here on the grass and eat my
ice-cream. It won't take long," he said
to himself.

It felt good sitting in the sun with no one
nagging him.

Then he made another mistake. He fell
asleep.

Chapter

4

Joe woke up with a jolt. He looked around him. How the hell could he let himself fall asleep at a time like this? And how long had he been asleep? He looked at his watch. An hour! He'd been asleep for an hour! Joe leapt to his feet.

He bent down to pick up his bag. His ice cream had melted all over it.

He grabbed the bag and ran. He tried to keep out of the way of prams and shopping baskets and dogs.

Why did people go so slowly when they were out shopping?

But where was he going? Where was the road to Liverpool? Joe ran until his legs and arms hurt. Then he slowed down and tried to think what to do.

He must get to the Liverpool road and get a lift before anyone came after him. He looked around. There was a roundabout a little way up the road. There must be a signpost there to tell him the way.

Yes, there it was! It said Liverpool to the right. He was about to cross to the other side of the road when he stopped. A woman just behind bumped into him.

"Can't you look where you're going?" she said. Joe didn't hear her.

His eyes were fixed on two policemen standing on the other side of the road.

It was clear to Joe that they were looking for someone. "Oh _____! It's me they're looking for," he said to himself.

He had no chance of getting a lift now. If he stood by the roadside the police would see him.

He felt like running. But he told himself not to panic. He had to train himself to put up with setbacks like this.

"Train! That's it. I'll take a train to Liverpool," he said to himself. He'd be safer on a train. He could sit down and be with lots of people. He wouldn't be so easily spotted. "Good thinking, Joe boy."

He asked a man in the street the way to the train station. Then he started walking. "Now take your time," he said to himself. "Take it slowly. People start looking if you rush around too much."

It wasn't long before he got to the railway station. It was a small station and there were only one or two people about. They were young people with rucksacks on their backs.

Joe went to the ticket desk. "One to Liverpool, please," he said.

"How old are you?" said the man at the desk.

"Why do you want to know?" asked Joe.

"Are you over 15?" asked the man.

"Yes," lied Joe.

"Well in that case, you'll have to pay the full fare.

"Oh hell," Joe said to himself. That was another mistake. He could have saved himself some money if he hadn't lied about his age. He handed over the money.

"Are you on your own?" asked the man.

Joe said, "Yes. I mean, well, someone's meeting me at the other end."

"Been on holiday here, have you?" asked the man.

"Yes. With my friend and his mum and dad. It was fun," said Joe.

The man said, "Well, the train to Liverpool will be here at 1.30 p.m. That's about one hour from now. If you want something to eat or drink you'll have to go to the café over the road. A lot of people go there and wait for the trains."

Joe didn't want to wait. He wanted to get on the train and be on his way to Liverpool. But there was nothing he could do about it.

"Thanks," said Joe. And off he went across the road to the café. The smell of food made him feel hungry.

"I'll have eggs, beans, chips and a cup of tea, please," he said to the girl.

Joe paid for the food and sat down by the window.

He was just dipping a chip into his egg when he saw two policemen go into the station.

Joe dropped his fork with a bang. The girl looked across at him but she didn't say anything. Joe picked up his bag. It was time to get going. The police must be on to him.

He dashed out of the café and into the crowds of people on the streets. He felt safer with people all around him.

He walked slowly and tried to think. The police were on the lookout for him so he couldn't get to Liverpool by road or rail today. He would have to stay around here.

But he didn't want to try to get a room for the night. A boy of his age asking for a room would look a bit odd. The best place for him was on the beach. It came to him in a flash. The cave! The cave he had been to with his dad.

Chapter 5

Joe sat in the cave looking out to sea.
The sun was going down and he was cold
and fed up.

When darkness came, fear came with it.
He had planned to be in Liverpool by
this time. But here he was, trapped in a
cold, damp cave with the police looking
for him.

Joe put his sleeping bag on the hard floor of the cave.

He got in and tried to get to sleep. But it was no good. It was much colder than last night. Even when he got right down into his sleeping bag he was still cold.

After a time he sat up and got out his gas stove. He felt around for the matches and lit it.

Then he sat with his hands close to the stove and the heat made him feel better. This time when he put his head down he fell asleep.

Then the dreams began. In his dream, Joe could see men with dogs. The dogs were on leads and the men were running quickly to keep up with them.

Sometimes the dogs would stop and sniff the ground. Then they would run on again, barking loudly.

Suddenly, one of the men shouted, "There he is! Over there!" Now Joe could see what they were hunting. It was a boy. And he was running as fast as he could. The boy stumbled and fell.

"Let the dogs have him!" shouted one of the men. The dogs were set free and they ran over the ground, barking louder than ever.

"Kill him, kill him!" shouted the men.

The boy tried to get away but the dogs were closing in for the kill. As the first dog reached him, the boy turned his head away from the sharp teeth. And for the first time in his dream, Joe could see the boy's face.

There was a scream as the dog sank its teeth into the boy's neck. And Joe sat up as he screamed himself awake.

He was the boy in the dream. It was him the men had been looking for. And they had found him.

Joe sat listening to the sounds of the night. He was shaking with fear. He told himself that dreams could frighten you, but they couldn't hurt you.

As he looked out of the cave, he saw a light on the sea. It was a light on a ship and it made him think of his dad.

Suddenly, he felt stronger. He got down into his sleeping bag and drifted off to sleep. But the dreams came back.

This time he was on his dad's ship. There was a loud bang as the ship hit rocks and began to sink. All around him people were jumping into the sea.

He shut his eyes and jumped. The ice-cold water took his breath away.

He swam to one of the lifeboats. He could see his dad reaching out a hand to help him.

But as he got to the boat his dad changed into Mr Barker.

And the hand wasn't trying to help him, it was pushing him under the water. He held his breath for as long as he could but his lungs were bursting. Water began seeping into his nose and mouth. He knew he was going to drown.

Then he woke up, gasping for air and wet with sweat.

Chapter 6

Joe lay in his sleeping bag. He was frightened and didn't want to fall asleep again.

"Come on," he said to himself. "You need to get some food inside you."

The sun was up, and light was coming into the cave. He reached out for the matches and tried to light the gas stove.

But it wouldn't light.

Oh, no! He had left the stove on when he had gone to sleep and the gas had run out. Now he had no way to cook his food. What was he going to do?

Joe sat looking out of the cave. "Now come on, think. You've got a brain in your head, so use it," he said to himself. Maybe there was something down on the beach he could use to make a fire.

Joe took a look outside. He didn't want anyone to see that he was living in the cave. He jumped down and ran along the beach trying to get warm. As he ran he looked for things he could use to make a fire.

He found bits of paper and wood. It made him feel better. He had made mistakes but he had to keep going.

Joe soon had an armful of things that would help make a fire. He began walking back to his cave.

He was feeling hungry. His last meal had been in the café. And he had left most of it on the plate.

He needed to get a fire going and get some beans cooking in a pan. He licked his lips just thinking about them.

But as he got close to his cave he got a shock. Somebody was coming out of his cave with the tins of food in his hands. Joe dropped the paper and wood and began to run.

"Hey you! Put that food down!" he shouted.

The lad jumped down from the cave and began running with the tins under his arm.

Joe ran after him. As he reached him he tackled him round the legs. They both crashed to the ground in a heap. The tins of food fell onto the sand.

Joe jumped on top of him and punched him as hard as he could.

Then he hit him again.

But the lad was stronger than him. He rolled over and grabbed Joe's arms. Joe struggled to get an arm free so he could punch him again. But the grip was too tight and he couldn't do it.

Then the lad pushed Joe sideways onto the sand. They got up and faced each other.

"That's my food you've got there. And you got it from my cave!" shouted Joe.

Joe was so angry that he ran at him again. The lad grabbed him and kicked his legs from under him.

Then he got Joe onto the ground and began pushing his head into the sand. Joe tried, but he couldn't get him off his back.

"Now stop fighting, or I'll push your face so far into the sand you won't get it out again," said the lad.

Joe tried one last time but it was no good. His face was being pushed deeper and deeper into the sand. He felt as if he was going to choke.

Chapter

7

Joe stopped fighting. The lad got off his back and let him get up. But he still kept a hand on his arm.

Joe pushed the hand away. Then he spat sand out of his mouth and tried to get his breath back.

He also tried to think about how he was going to hang on to his food.

Starting a fight again wasn't a good idea. The lad was about the same age as Joe but he was taller and bigger. Joe had to try something.

"So why did you steal my food?" asked Joe. "You've got no right taking my food."

The lad didn't say a word. He just bent down, picked up the tins of food and gave them back to Joe. Then he began walking off down the beach.

Joe didn't know what to do. "Hang on, wait a minute!" he shouted.

The lad stopped as Joe ran up to him.

"I don't get it," said Joe. You could have taken the tins. So why are you giving them back to me?"

The lad looked as if he was going to say something. But he began walking again.

Joe ran up to him. "Come on, tell me. Why did you take my food and then give it back to me?"

The lad said, "Look. I saw the tins in the cave and I needed food. But I'm not a thief. You've got them back. Now leave me alone." He began walking again.

"Did you say you were hungry?" asked Joe.

The lad stopped and nodded his head.

"Well, come back to the cave and I'll cook some beans," said Joe. The lad just stood there.

"Come on. Come and have some of it," said Joe.

The two of them went back to the cave. Joe picked up the wood and paper from the beach and made a fire. Then he cooked a pan of beans.

The lad just sat there, saying nothing. Joe put some of the cooked beans into a small dish and handed it to him. Then he ate the rest from the pan. They both gulped down their beans.

"Are you on holiday down here then?" asked the lad.

"No," said Joe.

"You live around here then, do you?" he asked.

"No," said Joe.

"So why are you living in a cave?" he asked. Joe didn't know what to say.

Then the lad asked, "Are you the kid the police are looking for? The one who has run away from home?"

Joe's mouth fell open. "It's got nothing to do with you. Stop asking me so many questions," he said.

The lad said, "OK, OK, keep your hair on. I'm not going to tell anyone. I've just run away from home too, so I'm keeping well away from the police."

Joe didn't know if he could trust him. "Have you really run away from home?" he asked.

"Yes," said the lad. "I'm trying to get to London so I can live with my brother.

"So how do you know the police are after me?" asked Joe.

"It's in the newspapers. I found one this morning and read it. Your name's Joe, isn't it?" said the lad.

Joe nodded his head. He was trying not to panic. Everyone seemed to be after him.

"What's your name?" asked Joe.

"Harry," said the lad.

"Why did you leave home?" asked Joe.

"Well," said Harry. "My dad died and my mum got married again. I don't like my new stepdad and he doesn't like me. We just end up arguing all the time. I can't stand living in the same house as him. So I'm off to London to stay with my brother. What about you?" Harry asked.

Joe told him all about his dad. Then the two of them sat looking into the fire.

At last, Harry said, "Look Joe, I've got to get going. I've got to get out of town before the police start asking me questions. I slept in a shelter by the beach last night and someone may have spotted me. Your story being in the paper will mean more people are on the lookout for runaways. I wish we could help each other. But you're going to Liverpool and I'm off to London."

Harry got to his feet. Then he said, "There is one thing I can help you with. Keep your eyes open for a gang of older lads. I've seen them steal things from shops and chase kids on the beach. So look after yourself."

They both went outside the cave.

"Thanks for the food, Joe. It was just what I needed," said Harry.

He took a small bottle of water out of his pocket and took a drink. He handed the rest to Joe.

"Keep it. I can get some more."
He jumped down onto the sand. "I hope you find your dad, Joe. And whatever you do, don't give up," said Harry.

Then off he went down the beach.

"Good luck!" shouted Joe.

Chapter

8

Joe went back into the cave and sat by the
fire. He had some more thinking to do.
The sun was getting higher in the sky and
there would soon be people all over town.
How many of them would have read the
morning paper? How was he going to get
to Liverpool without being spotted as a
runaway? And when should he get going?

He sat back against the wall of the cave and tried to work things out. He was warm from the fire and food. And tired from fighting.

He shut his eyes and was soon fast asleep. The sun rose even higher. The town filled up with people and cars. Men and women rushed to work. Shops opened.

And a gang of lads made their way along the beach!

Joe was still fast asleep. He didn't see the gang kicking a football to each other. He didn't see one of them kick the ball up into the rocks next to his cave.

And he didn't see him come up the rocks to get the ball.

But he did wake up when the gang came into his cave. He got to his feet as fast as he could.

One of the gang said, "My name's Rick. What's your name, boy?"

"Get lost," said Joe.

Rick's fist hit Joe on the side of his head. He fell back onto the wall of the cave.

"I said, what's your name?" snarled Rick. Joe told him his name.

"That's better," said Rick.

Rick looked around the cave. Then he looked at one of the gang.

"Well, what have we got here? What do you think it is, Gaz?" he said.

Gaz wasn't as tall as Rick but he had a mean-looking face. He looked at Joe's things in the cave and said, "I think we've got a right little gold mine, Rick. We should get plenty of cash for this little lot," said Gaz.

Rick picked up Joe's sleeping bag. "Yes," he said. "We should get plenty of cash."

Joe grabbed his sleeping bag off him and made a dash for it. But it was no good. Rick was too fast for him.

He grabbed him by the arm and said, "Not so fast, you. You're not going anywhere. Not until we've finished with you."

Two of the lads held onto Joe, as Rick had a good look round the cave.

"Now then," said Rick. "What have we got?" He picked up the gas stove. "One stove. I can sell this."

Then he grabbed the sleeping bag from Joe. "And get a quid or two for this."

Joe tried to get his arms free but it was no good.

Rick looked at Joe's watch. "I'll have that. It's only cheap but I'll get something for it," he said.

Then he put his face next to Joe's. "Now, now. If you try and get away from us I'll have to belt you again," he said.

Rick picked up Joe's bag and threw out the clothes.

"Just what I need to put the stove and sleeping bag in. Thanks Joe. I'm glad we met you," he said.

Joe hoped they wouldn't see his jacket and his bottle with a ship in it.

"Now then," said Rick. "Let's see if I've missed anything. We wouldn't want to miss anything, would we?"

Rick looked round the cave. Then he saw Joe's jacket. He picked it up and felt in the pockets.

"What a shame, no mobile. But what have we got here?" said Rick. Joe tried to get free but the boys held onto him.

Rick took the money out of the pocket and counted it.

"There's over £80 here. Thank you, Joe. This is just what we need."

Joe wished he was bigger and could fight them off. But all he could do was stand and watch as they stole from him.

Rick dropped the jacket and handed out the money. "Some for you, Gaz. Some for you three. And even more for me. Oh dear, Joe. I don't think there's any money left for you," he said.

The gang sneered and laughed.

"Well, Joe. Thanks for having us. I do hope we meet again," said Rick.

The gang were just leaving when Rick said, "Hang on. What's that down there?"

Joe tried to get there first but Rick pushed him to one side. Then he picked up the bottle with the ship in it.

"I nearly missed this," said Rick.

Joe yelled out, "Please don't take that! My dad gave it to me. Please don't take it." But Rick put the bottle in the bag. And the gang pushed Joe to the back of the cave.

"See you, Joe!" they shouted. Then they jumped down onto the sand, kicking the football as they went down the beach.

Joe just sat in the cave. He knew there was nothing he could do about it.

Chapter

9

Joe didn't know what he was going to do.
The gang had taken everything he had.
They had even taken the present from his
dad. He felt lonely, fed up and angry.

After a time, he got up and sat outside
the cave. The people on the beach were
packing up. He knew they would be going
home for a drink and a meal.

He wanted to go with them and be looked after. He began thinking about Harry.

"I bet he's OK," Joe said to himself. "I bet he's in London by now."

But as he sat there, he began to think about what Harry had said to him, "Whatever you do, don't give up."

The words kept going around inside his head. "Don't give up, don't give up."

Joe banged his fist on the ground. No, he wouldn't give up. He had run away to find his dad and he was going to keep on looking. He had to know what happened to him.

He went back into the cave and looked around. He still had a box of matches, a pan, a tin opener and a tin of beans. The gang hadn't taken everything after all. He got to work and made a fire.

He cooked the beans and sat looking out to sea as he ate them.

His dad loved beans. He used to slurp them down with a spoon. Then he'd mop up with a big chunk of bread. Joe would get his fingers tapped with the spoon if he tried nicking any.

The sky was turning red as the sun seemed to drop into the sea. It would soon be dark. Joe put his last bit of wood on the fire. It was going to be a cold night without his sleeping bag.

He stayed by the fire until it went out. Then he tried to keep warm by jumping up and down and running on the spot. But as soon as he stopped he got cold again.

He didn't think it got so cold at night. His teeth started chattering and his fingers went numb. The cold seemed to get right into his bones. There was no chance of getting any sleep.

As the night went on, Joe felt as if he was going to freeze to death.

And the colder he got, the more gloomy
he became. He didn't want to give up
looking for his dad, but it was hopeless
doing it like this.

How was he going to keep going without
money? What would he do when his food
ran out? Would the gang come back?

He didn't want to give up. But what else
could he do?

As Joe sat shaking with cold, he made up
his mind. As soon as the sun came up he
would go to the police.

The sound of a police car made him
jump. Were they coming for him?

He rushed outside to have a look. But
the cars were not stopping by the beach.
They were racing into town. And now Joe
could see why they were going so fast.

A fire was blazing in the town. Red
and yellow flames were leaping into the
night sky.

The flames were getting bigger and clouds of smoke were blotting out the stars.

"Wow. That's going to take a long time to put out," Joe said to himself.

Then came the sound of fire engines as they raced along the road with all lights flashing. There were going to be some tired firemen before that blaze was put out.

Joe didn't stay watching the fire for long. It was even colder outside the cave than in.

He went back inside, wishing he could bring some of the fire with him. He huddled in the cave and waited for the morning.

Chapter 10

After a long night, the sky turned to a
pale shade of red. Joe got to his feet.
It was time to go. He was freezing cold
and his legs were stiff. And he was angry
with himself.

His plan to run away from the Barkers
had seemed a good one. But he hadn't got
to Liverpool.

All he'd done was travel 12 miles and spend one night in a barn and two nights in a cave. Now he was walking along the beach and giving himself up to the police. He stopped and skimmed some pebbles on the sea. He saw two ships far away.

"I will try again, Dad. Honest I will," he said.

He walked along the beach until he came to the streets of the town. There was no one about. He didn't know where the police station was so he just kept on walking.

But as he went round the next corner he saw them. Policemen! Lots of them.

They were looking at the mess the fire had made. The roof of a big shop had come down but the brick walls were still standing. Everything was black, and smoke was still rising from the ashes.

There was glass and water everywhere.

Joe stood still. His heart was beating fast. The policemen hadn't seen him yet. He still had time to run away again.

No! He had made up his mind. He may as well get on with it. He went up to one of the policemen.

"Yes son, what can I do for you?" asked the policeman.

"It's about the runaway boy," said Joe.

The policeman looked at him and said, "Yes, a sad thing that. A fireman found him as they were putting out the fire. They just couldn't get him out in time."

Joe stood and looked at the policeman. "You mean, you've found the boy that ran away from home?" he said.

The policeman said, "Yes. I've just told you. A fireman found his body. He should never have been in the shop. We don't know what he was doing in there. But he must have got trapped in the fire."

Joe didn't know what to say. He was in shock. He knew the police had made a mistake.

"But how do you know it was the boy who ran away from home?" asked Joe.

The policeman seemed to be getting fed up with his questions.

"We know it was the boy because we found what's left of some of his things. We found part of his bag, a scrap of his sleeping bag, and a camping stove. We also found what we think was a ship in a bottle. And we know he had that with him," he said.

Joe just stood with his mouth open.

"Come on lad. We have a lot of work to do here. Get yourself out of the way," said the policeman.

Joe walked away from the crowd and tried to think. The police had made a big mistake.

It must have been one of the gang that had been killed. And that would mean the police wouldn't be on the lookout for a runaway boy. He was free!

Joe went on down the street. But how long had he got before the police found out that they had made a mistake? And he still had no money, no food, and only the clothes he stood up in. And he had nowhere to stay.

He knew he couldn't spend another night in a cold cave. He sat on a wall and tried to think. As he sat, he began looking in his pockets. He was hoping to find some money that the gang had missed.

There was no money. But there was something in the top pocket of his jacket. It was a ticket. It was his train ticket to Liverpool!

The police had come to the station before he had got on the train.

He could still use it. He could still get to Liverpool. But where would he stay? How would he eat?

Joe looked across at the sea. Then he looked down at the ticket in his hand. Was it time to take a risk? Or was it time to go back?

He put the ticket back in his top pocket. Then he jumped down from the wall, and walked up the street to the railway station . . .

Joe's story continues in

The Boss

Turn the page for a preview . . .

SURVIVAL

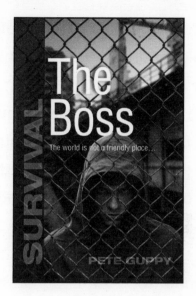

The Boss

The world is not a friendly place...

SURVIVAL

PETE GUPPY

Joe looked to his left. Then he looked to his right. He was trapped.

The walls were too big to get over and the gang were closing in.

They were standing in a line across the road, walking slowly towards him. They didn't need to rush. They knew they had him trapped.

There were six of them. And they all looked bigger and older than him. There was only one thing to do. He ran at the gang and tried pushing past them.

It was no good. Strong arms stopped him and pushed him back against the wall.

"Not so fast. I want a word with you," said the leader of the gang.

"_____ off," said Joe.

The leader took off his sunglasses. He was much older than the others.

"Now look. There's an easy way of doing this, and there's a hard way. It's up to you," he said.

Joe was shaking with fear but he said, "Get lost. Leave me alone."

The gang leader got so close that Joe could smell he'd been drinking. He could also see a long scar on the man's face. It went from his chin, across his cheek, and over to his left ear.

Scarface looked mean and hard.

"I haven't seen you around here before. What's your name?" he asked.

Joe didn't say a word.

This time, Scarface prodded Joe in the chest with his finger. "I said, what's your name? And what are you doing on my patch?"

Joe looked at the scar. "My name's Joe. And I'm looking for my dad," he said.

"That's better. Now tell me more," said Scarface.

"My dad works on the boats. He should have come home two years ago. I've run away to look for him. I've got to get on a boat to Hong Kong," said Joe.

"And have you got a ticket to get on a boat to Hong Kong?" asked Scarface.

"No," said Joe.

"Have you got the cash to buy a ticket?" asked Scarface.

"No," said Joe.

"So how are you going to get to Hong Kong?" asked Scarface.

"I don't know. I haven't worked that out, yet," said Joe.

Scarface looked at the gang. "Well, Joe, this is your lucky day. I think I can help you," he said. Then he asked Joe two more questions:

"Do you need some food?"

"Yes," said Joe.

"Do you need a bed for the night?"

"Yes," said Joe.

"Well, I think we can do a deal. You come and work for me and I'll get you to Hong Kong. What do you say?" asked Scarface.

Joe didn't know what to say. He didn't like the look of this man. But he did want to find his dad. And he was hungry.

Scarface said, "Come on. We'll look

after you. We'll get you some food and show you where you can sleep."

Then he turned to the gang and said, "Take Joe to the flat and get him some fish and chips. I'll see you later."

Joe let himself be led along the road by the gang. He couldn't fight them, or outrun them. He needed food and sleep. And maybe Scarface would keep to his word.

As they went up the road they looked just like a set of lads having fun. But the truth isn't always easy to see.

They came out of the back street and turned left into a park. Some boys were playing football and the gang kicked their ball away as they walked across the pitch.

At the end of the park they took a path leading to a block of flats.

When they got there, one of the gang looked around. Then they rushed up to the main doors.

A mum with a pram opened the doors from the inside. The gang pushed past her and ran with Joe up the steps to the second floor.

One of the gang unlocked the door of number 38 and they all went in.

"Well, here we are. Home sweet home," he said to Joe.

And the door was slammed shut . . .

Look out for other exciting stories in the
Survival series:

Runaway

The Boss

The Gambling Habit

Stormy Waters

Flirting with Danger

Fireproof

Why Me?

Jet Scream

Why Me?

'The gang saw him run, and gave a cheer. Showing fear was just what they wanted to see. It fed their hunger for power.'

When Wayne starts a new school his life is made hell by a group of bullies.

Will they beat him down, or can he fight back?

Fireproof

"I'll burn this school down one day. You see if I don't."

When Jack's school burns down that night the police come looking for him.

But did he do it?

Jet Scream

Day 1 . . .
The 52 people sitting on the plane knew they were going to die.

Ben and Jane are the only survivors of the plane crash. Will they be able to stay alive?

Flirting with Danger

Amrit and Jenny get their first taste of freedom as they head off on a backpacking trip away from their families.

But the fun soon turns to fear . . .

SURVIVAL

Stormy Waters

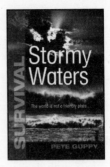

"I'm glad I don't fit in here. I hate rich people like you," yelled Nick.

Nick wants revenge. He takes Tim's boat but the prank soon turns into a nightmare.

How will the nightmare end?

The Gambling Habit

Gambling is the best feeling in the world for Steve. He's lying, stealing and shoplifting from one bet to the next.

What will it take to show him that there is more to life than gambling?

Runaway

Is Joe's dad still alive?

After no word from his dad for two years, Joe decides to go to the last place his dad was seen: Hong Kong.

Joe's story continues in 'The Boss'.

The Boss

Alone and afraid in Liverpool, Joe gets involved with a gang of drug pushers.

With no money, food or shelter Joe is an easy target for The Boss.

Joe's story begins in 'Runaway'.

SURVIVAL

About the author

Have you ever been hunted by the police, chased by a gang, or tried to stay alive after a plane crash?

If you have, then you know the name of the game is survival. If you haven't, why not read about the teenagers in my stories. They find getting into trouble is easy. It's the getting out of trouble that's the hard bit.

I spent three years training to be a teacher and 33 years being one.
I always wanted to know how hard it would be to write books for teenagers. Now I know!

Pete Guppy

SURVIVAL

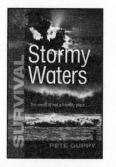

RISING ★ STARS

The Survival titles are available from most booksellers.

For more information please call Rising Stars on

0800 091 1602

or visit

www.risingstars-uk.com

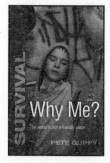